Little Red Riding Hood

Retold by Susanna Davidson

Based on a story by The Brothers Grimm

Illustrated by Mike Gordon

Once upon a time there was a little girl called Little Red Riding Hood.

She always wore a bright red cloak
with a bright red hood.

I love my cloak!

She lived with her mother in a cottage
on the edge of some deep, dark woods.

One day, Little Red Riding Hood's mother gave her a pot of Brussels sprout soup.

Rules of the Woods
1 • Keep to the path
2 • Don't talk to wolves

"Take this to your grandmother on the other side of the woods," she said.

"But remember the Rules of the Woods!"

"I promise," said Little Red Riding Hood, and off she went...

Skippety-skippety, skip. Skippety-skippety, skip.

"Oh what a lovely day!" said Little Red Riding Hood.

"Good morning, Little Red Riding Hood,"
called the woodcutter.

"Good morning, Woodcutter," called Little Red Riding Hood.

Little Red Riding Hood walked deeper and deeper into the deep, dark woods.

It grew darker and darker.

So Little Red Riding Hood didn't see
the wolf waiting for her on the path.

And the wolf didn't see Little Red Riding Hood either.

Little Red Riding Hood
stumbled
straight
into the wolf.

"What are you doing in the middle of the path?"
asked Little Red Riding Hood.
　　"I nearly spilled my grandmother's Brussels sprout soup."

Sprouts! Yuck!
Wolves only eat
JUICY RED
MEAT!

Little Red Riding Hood had forgotten the rule
　　　　　　　　　　–Don't talk to wolves.

The wolf was just about to gobble up
Little Red Riding Hood, when he had a BRILLIANT idea.

I'll eat Little Red Riding Hood
AND
her grandmother!

"And where does dear little Granny live?"
asked the wolf.

"In the cottage on the other side
of the woods," said Little Red Riding Hood.

The wolf raced to the cottage and knocked on the door.

TAP!

TAP!

TAP!

"Come in," called Grandmother.

The wolf leaped into the room...

...and gobbled up Little Red Riding Hood's grandmother in two seconds flat.

Mmm! Bony, but not bad.

Then he pulled on her cap, jumped into bed and waited for Little Red Riding Hood.

Soon, there was a knock at the door.

TAP!   TAP!   TAP!   "Come in," snarled the wolf,
as softly as he could.

Little Red Riding Hood looked
at her grandmother...

...then looked again.

In one bound, the wolf was out of bed
and gobbling up Little Red Riding Hood.

"Dee-licious!" he said...

...then fell fast asleep.

As he slept, he snored
-very **loudly**.

"What's going on?"
wondered the woodcutter.

"He's eaten that poor old woman!" realized the woodcutter.
He picked up some scissors.

He snipped open
the wolf's tummy.

Snippety-snip
Snippety-snip

Out popped Grandmother,
    and Little Red Riding Hood, too.

Quick as a flash, Little Red Riding Hood
picked up some stones and piled them
into the wolf's tummy.

When the wolf woke up, he tried to sneak out the door.

RATTLE
RATTLE
RATTLE

But the stones rattled and rattled and rattled inside him.

"Now everyone can hear me coming.
I'll never catch anyone," cried the wolf.

"Exactly!" said the woodcutter.

"You'll just have to eat vegetables instead,"
said Little Red Riding Hood.

The wolf was never able
to eat another person.

Urgh! Brussels
sprout soup.

As for Little Red Riding Hood,
she never, ever talked to a wolf again.

Edited by Jenny Tyler and Lesley Sims

Designed by Louise Flutter

Digital illustration by Carl Gordon